# Wasp
# or Bee
## Which Is Which?

By Tamra B. Orr

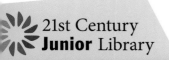
21st Century
**Junior** Library

Published in the United States of America by
**Cherry Lake Publishing**
Ann Arbor, Michigan
www.cherrylakepublishing.com

Reading Adviser: Marla Conn, MS, Ed., Literacy specialist, Read-Ability, Inc.
Content Adviser: Susan Heinrichs Gray

Photo Credits: ©aDam Wildlife/Shutterstock, cover (left), 4; ©manuk R/Shutterstock, cover (right);
©D. A. Boyd/Shutterstock, 6; ©Diyana Dimitrova/Shutterstock, 8; ©fotorobs/Shutterstock, 10;
©TravelPhotoSpirit/Shutterstock, 12; ©R K Hill/Shutterstock, 14; ©Mirko Graul/Shutterstock, 16;
©Neil Bromhall/Shutterstock, 18; ©Pxhere/Public Domain, 20

Library of Congress Cataloging-in-Publication Data

Names: Orr, Tamra, author.
Title: Wasp or bee / Tamra B. Orr.
Description: Ann Arbor : Cherry Lake Publishing, [2019] | Series: Which is which? | Includes bibliographical
    references and index. | Audience: K to Grade 3.
Identifiers: LCCN 2019006013 | ISBN 9781534147379 (hardcover) | ISBN 9781534150232 (paperback) |
    ISBN 9781534148802 (pdf) | ISBN 9781534151666 (hosted ebook)
Subjects: LCSH: Wasps—Juvenile literature. | Bees—Juvenile literature.
Classification: LCC QL565.2 .O77 2019 | DDC 595.79—dc23
LC record available at https://lccn.loc.gov/2019006013

Cherry Lake Publishing would like to acknowledge the work of the Partnership for 21st Century Skills.
Please visit *www.p21.org* for more information.

Printed in the United States of America
Corporate Graphics

# CONTENTS

A honeybee will visit anywhere between 50 to 100 flowers
in one single trip!

# A Buzzing Sound

Sssssssh! Do you hear that buzzing sound? Take a look around. Is there a wasp or a bee flying nearby? You spot the insect landing on the arm of a lawn chair. But is it a wasp or a bee? Sometimes it's difficult to tell which is which!

Both wasps and bees are flying, stinging insects. They have two pairs of wings. They

Wasps come in almost every color you can imagine, from yellow
to brown to even metallic blue and bright red!

both can have yellow and black patterns on their bodies. So it is easy to confuse the two.

Wasps and bees are found on every **continent** except Antarctica. There are 20,000 different types of bees in the world. But there are nearly 100,000 types of wasps. The bees most familiar to people are honey-bees and bumble bees. The wasps you're likely to see are yellow jackets and hornets.

In a hive, there are three types of bee roles:
the queen, drones, and worker bees.

Telling the difference between these insects would be easier if you could see them up close. Honeybees and bumblebees have plump, fuzzy bodies. Wasps tend to have slender, smooth bodies. Bees have flat, hairy rear legs for holding on to pollen as they fly. The wasps' legs are hairless. Both insects buzz because of how fast their wings are beating.

# Make a Guess!

A bumblebee's buzz is especially loud when it lands on a flower. It is **vibrating** its wing and **thorax** muscles. This action shakes the pollen off the flower and onto the bee's body. What do you think it will do next?

There are two types of wasps: social and solitary.

# Ouch! That Stings

Another thing bees and wasps have in common is their stingers. How and why they use these natural weapons differs, though. A bee's main purpose in life is to **pollinate**. It is usually a peaceful insect. Bees tend to only sting if they feel threatened. Honeybees can only sting once. This bee can't pull its **barbed** stinger out of a person's skin. When it flies away, it leaves its stinger behind. The bee also leaves parts of its insides behind. Stinging a person will kill the bee.

A hive of bees needs to travel about 55,000 miles (88,514 kilometers) visiting flowers to make 1 pound (0.45 kilogram) of honey.

Wasps are far more **aggressive** than bees. Like bees, females are the only ones that can sting. And they are quick to sting anything they see as a threat. Their stingers are not barbed, so they can be used again and again. This means wasps can sting repeatedly. They are **predators**, and will go after other insects.  They also eat nectar and sugary foods. So don't leave anything out after your picnic lunch!

# Ask Questions!

Getting stung hurts. But do not try to fight back by attacking it. A yellow jacket or honeybee might have a nest close by. A bee under attack will send out a special **scent**. This tells the bee's friends and family that it is in trouble. They will immediately head toward you to get even!

Most common wasps have a slim "waist" unlike bees.

# Nests and Hives

Wasps and bees build very different homes. Bees use their wax **glands** to create a hive. The honeybee hive is made out of six-sided wax cells stacked on top of each other. Worker bees build these colonies for all the bees to live in. They store honey, raise baby bees, and take care of the queen bee. Some of these hives have as many as 75,000 insects inside them. Honeybee hives are usually built in tree holes or empty

Young honeybees are taught how to make honey by older bees.

buildings. Bumble bees often build on or under the ground.

Wasps do not have wax glands. The wasps find old wood, like that found on fences and porches. They chew off pieces and mix them with their **saliva**. This creates a paper-like paste. They use it to build papery nests in hidden or protected spots. You'll see these nests under decks, on porches, or in cracked concrete. Some wasps even build their nests underground.

# Look!

Not everyone puts up with hornets. In some parts of the world, people eat them! Some prefer them raw, while others like them fried. There are even recipes for adding them to cracker dough.

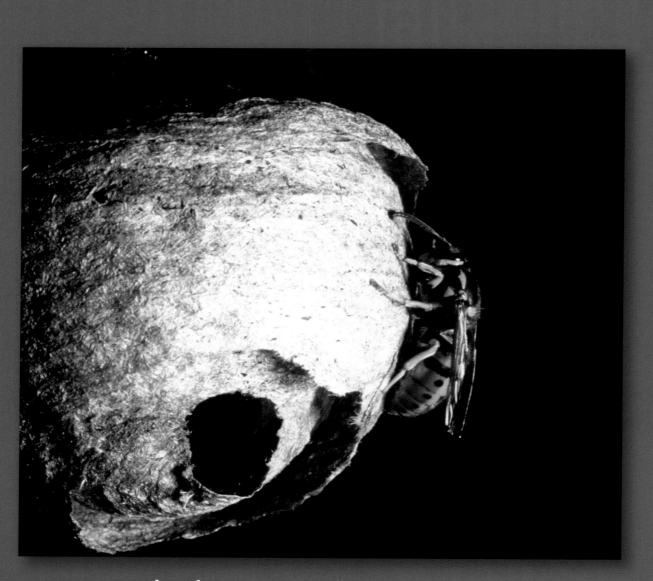

Except for a few new queens, all wasps die during the fall.

# An Insect's Purpose

Bee and wasp homes aren't just made differently. What they do is different too. During the winter, most queen wasps **hibernate** until warm weather returns. Just before fall ends, they tend to be more aggressive. They are searching for tasty insects to eat. They want to fill up before the long months of hibernation begin. Some types of bees hibernate, while others do not. For example, bumblebees hibernate. But honeybees stay awake all winter, keeping warm inside the hive.

While worker bees die after stinging, queen bees
can sting multiple times without dying.

When spring comes around again, both insects get busy. Bees are responsible for pollinating fruit trees, vegetable plants, and flowers. They keep gardens growing! Wasps are hungry **carnivores**. They do a great job of controlling the populations of crickets, flies, and caterpillars.

Wasps and bees are amazing insects. Give them plenty of room and watch from afar. You don't want to risk getting stung!

# Ask Questions!

During its lifetime, a single honeybee will only make 0.08 teaspoon (0.4 milliliter) of honey. That's less than ¼ teaspoon! How many honeybees would it take to make 1 tablespoon (15 mL)? How about an entire jar?

# GLOSSARY

**aggressive** (uh-GRES-iv) ready or likely to attack

**barbed** (BARBD) having a sharp point that sticks out and backward from a larger point

**carnivores** (KAHR-nuh-vorz) animals that eat meat

**continent** (KAHN-tuh-nuhnt) one of seven large landmasses of the earth

**glands** (GLANDZ) clusters of cells or organs in bodies that produce a substance, like saliva, to be used by the body

**hibernate** (HYE-bur-nate) spend the winter sleeping or resting

**pollinate** (PAH-luh-nate) carry pollen to and from a flower or plant so it will produce seeds

**predators** (PRED-uh-turz) animals that live by hunting other animals for food

**saliva** (suh-LYE-vuh) the watery liquid in your mouth that keeps it moist

**scent** (SENT) smell

**thorax** (THOR-aks) middle section of the body of an insect

**vibrating** (VYE-brayt-ing) moving back and forth very quickly

# FIND OUT MORE

## BOOKS

Hamilton, S. L. *Bees and Wasps.* Minneapolis, MN: A&D Xtreme, 2015.

Latta, Sara. *Bees and Wasps: Secrets of Their Busy Colonies.* North Mankato, MN: Capstone Press, 2019.

Rockwood, Leigh. *Tell Me the Difference Between a Bee and a Wasp.* New York, NY: PowerKids Press, 2013.

Sirota, Lyn. *Insects as Pollinators.* Vero Beach, FL: Rourke Educational Media, 2016.

## WEBSITES

**CBC Kids—Bee or Wasp?**
https://www.cbc.ca/kidscbc2/the-feed/bee-or-wasp
Read more about the differences between bees and wasps.

**YouTube—The Biggest Difference Between Wasps and Bees**
https://www.youtube.com/watch?v=r_d4RdLQaDw
Discover more fascinating facts about these buzzing insects.

# INDEX

## ABOUT THE AUTHOR

Tamra Orr is the author of hundreds of books for readers of all ages. She graduated from Ball State University, but moved with her husband and four children to Oregon in 2001. She is a full-time author, and when she isn't researching and writing, she writes letters to friends all over the world. Orr enjoys life in a suburb of Portland, where she has a wasp nest on her deck that she watches through the window.